# Spaceboy Finds a Friend

Story by Michèle Dufresne
Illustrations by Tatjana Mai-Wyss

PIONEER VALLEY EDUCATIONAL PRESS, INC.

"Goodbye, Mom," said Spaceboy.
"I'm going to Earth
to find a friend."

Spaceboy landed on Earth.
He jumped out of his spaceship
and looked around.

"Oh, look!" said Spaceboy.
"Earth is all white."

"And look!
Here is a friend for me!"
said Spaceboy.

"Hello, Earthboy," said Spaceboy.
"Will you be my friend?
Hello! **Hello!** **Hello!**"

"He can't be your friend.
He's just a snowman,"
said a boy.

"Oh," said Spaceboy.
He looked sad.

"But I will be your friend,"
said the boy.

"Come on," said the boy.
"You can help me make
another snowman."